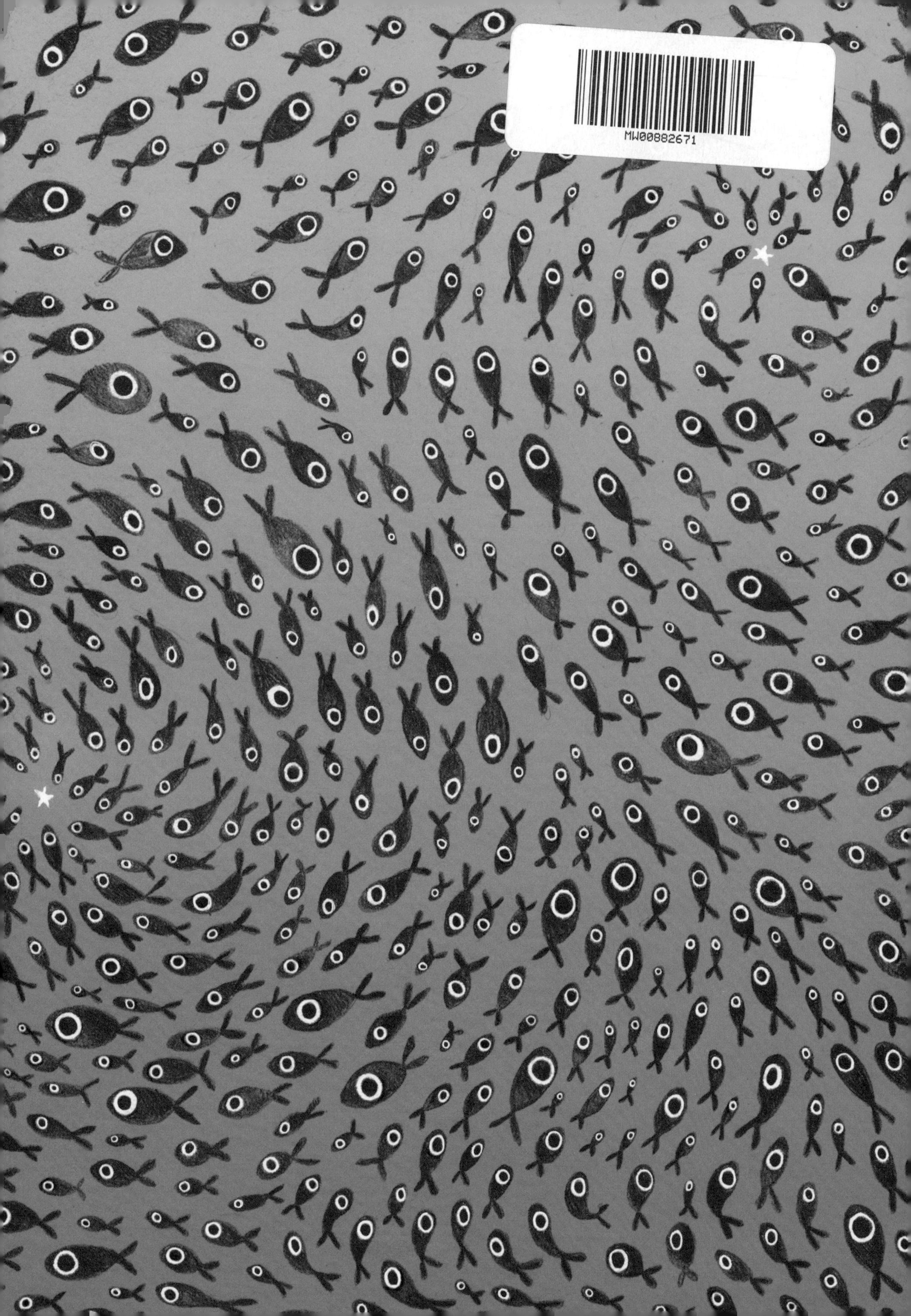
MW00882671

For David and Daisy, my Lucky stars.

Published by Sellers Publishing, Inc.


Sellers Publishing, Inc.
161 John Roberts Road, South Portland, Maine 04106
Visit our website: www.sellerspublishing.com
E-mail: rsp@rsvp.com

Charlotte Cromwell, Production Editor

ISBN 13: 978-1-5319-1481-3

Library of Congress Control Number: 2020943717


10 9 8 7 6 5 4 3 2 1

Printed in China.

Lucky
ERIN BROWN

A little girl and her mom went for a boat ride
to watch whales swim in the sea.

Lucky, her toy elephant, happily sat in the girl's lap.

Suddenly, a large wave swept over the boat and Lucky slipped out of the little girl's grasp.

She called out for help, but it was too late.
Lucky was swept overboard.

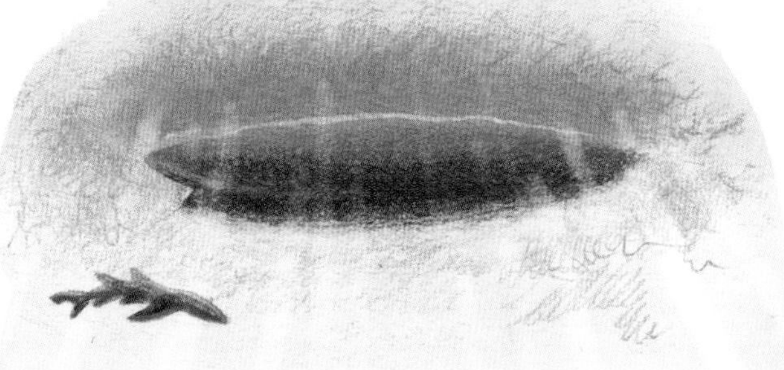

The little girl, her mom, and the Captain of the boat couldn't do anything but watch as Lucky sank down, down, down deep into the water.

A seal saw Lucky in the water.
It caught Lucky and brought
him to play with his friends.

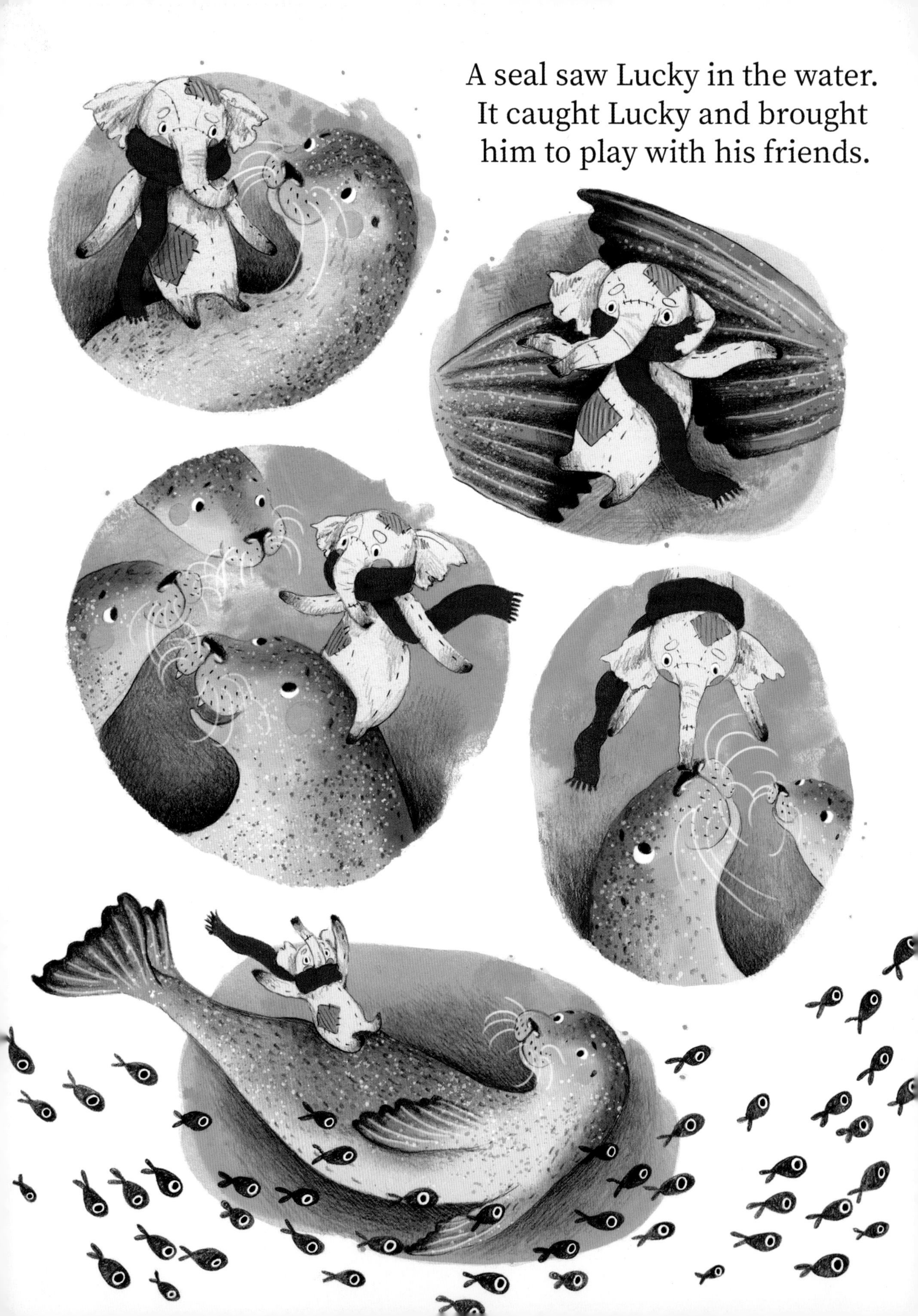

They swam all around Lucky,
swirling and twirling in the water.

But something startled the seals
and they swam away.
A shark!

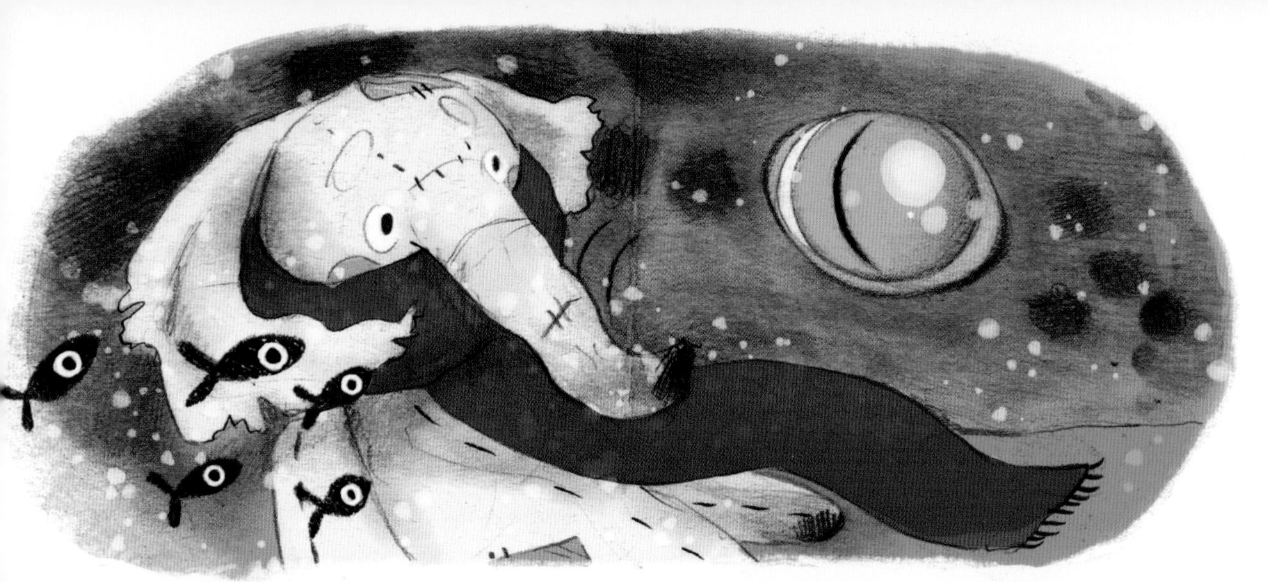

Lucky wondered if the shark was friendly or dangerous. Before he could decide, something wrapped around his leg and pulled him downward.

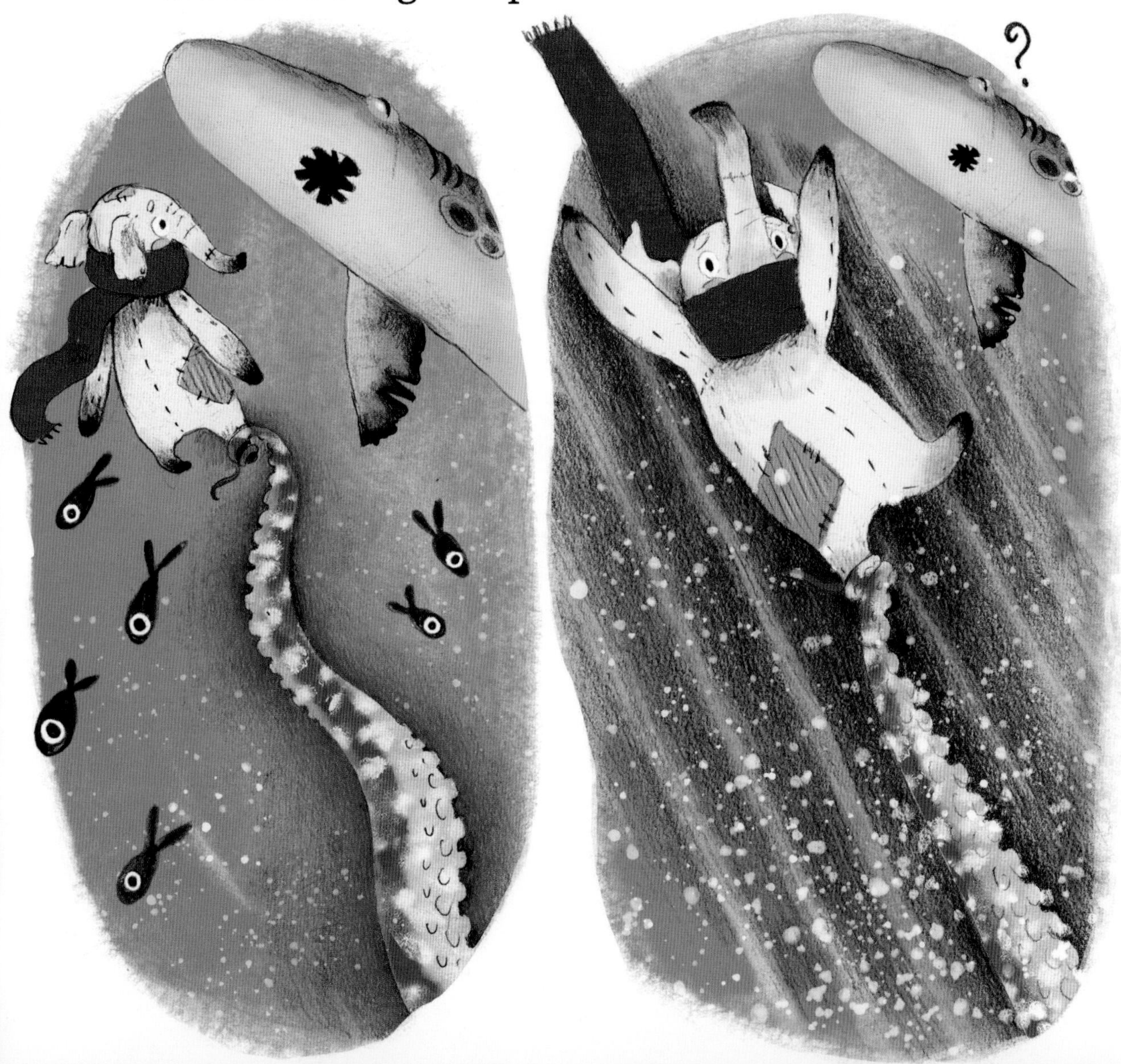

An octopus!

Lucky was pulled down,
down,
down,
even deeper into the sea
by the curious octopus.

It hugged Lucky tightly.

The shark came back

and Lucky disappeared
into a cloud of ink!

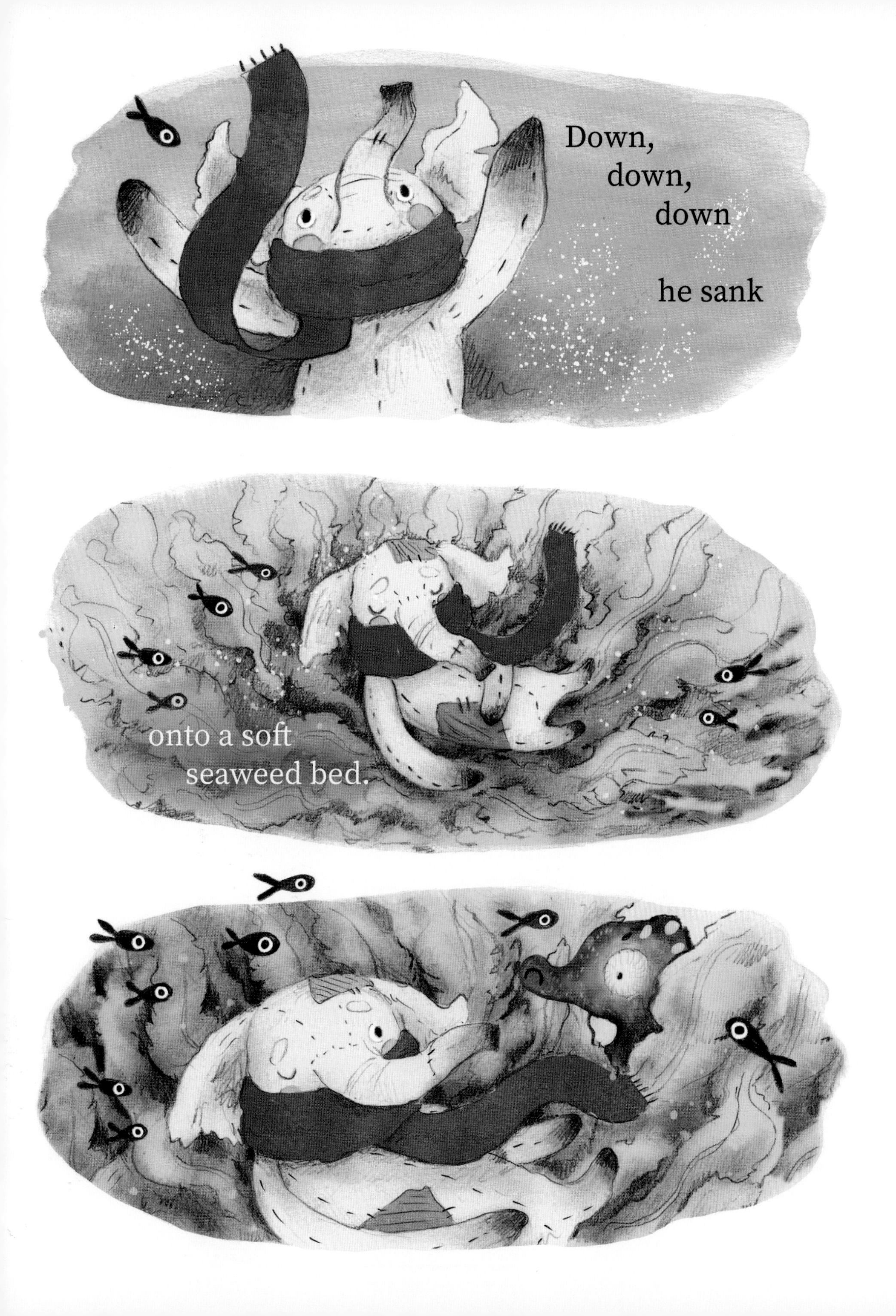
Down,
down,
down
he sank
onto a soft
seaweed bed.

Some seahorses lived
in the seaweed.

They became upset that Lucky
was in their home and gently
pushed him out.

He sank down,
down,
down
deeper into the water
until he landed on
the sea floor.

On the sea floor he lay thinking about the little girl. Oh how he missed her and how very alone he was.

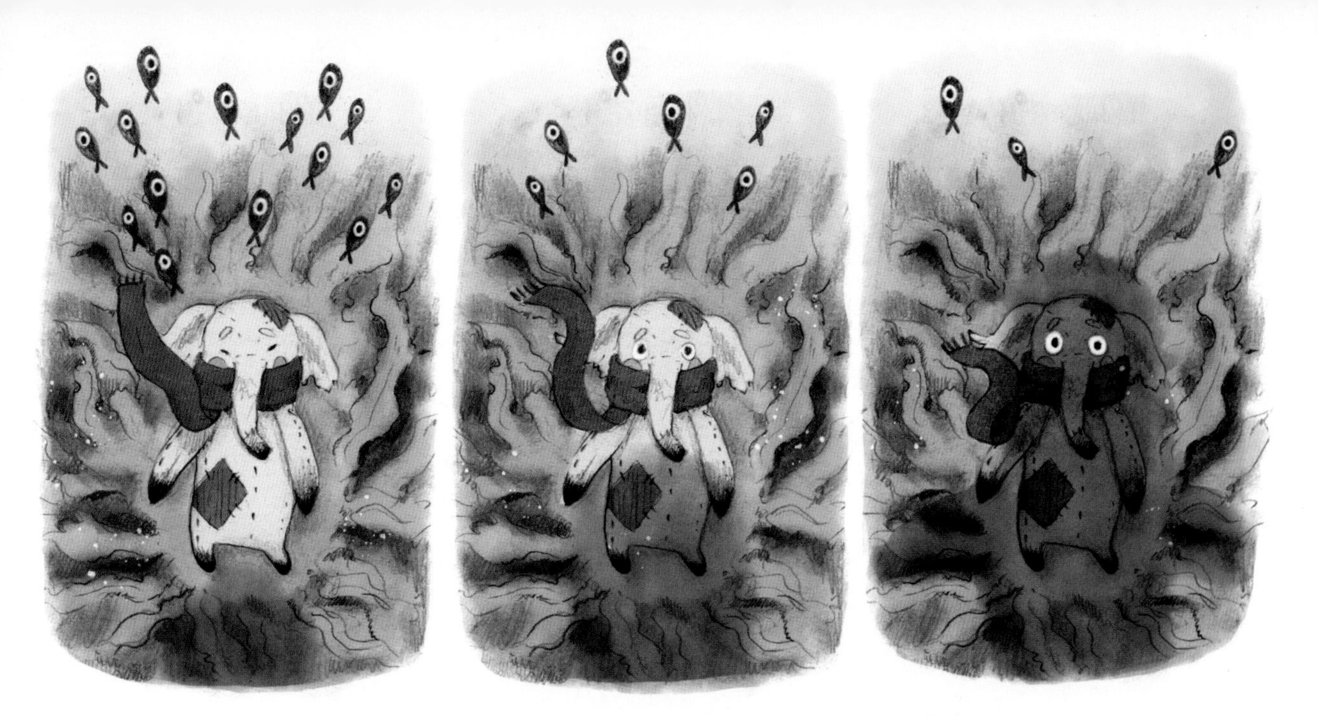

His thoughts were interrupted by
a dark shadow that swept over him.

The shark!

Lucky became frightened
and covered his eyes,

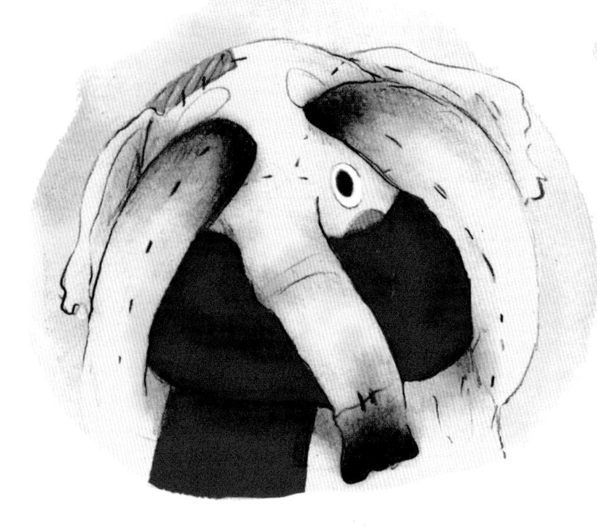

but nothing happened.

Lucky knew at that moment that the shark was friendly!

The shark had seen Lucky
fall from the boat, and he
had an idea about how he could
help Lucky get home.

The shark pulled Lucky
up, up, up
towards a whale that
was swimming near the
boat Lucky had fallen
from the day before.

The shark pulled Lucky up and over the top of the whale

and dropped him right over the whale's blowhole!

The whale released a huge breath
of air through its blowhole and
Lucky soared upwards!

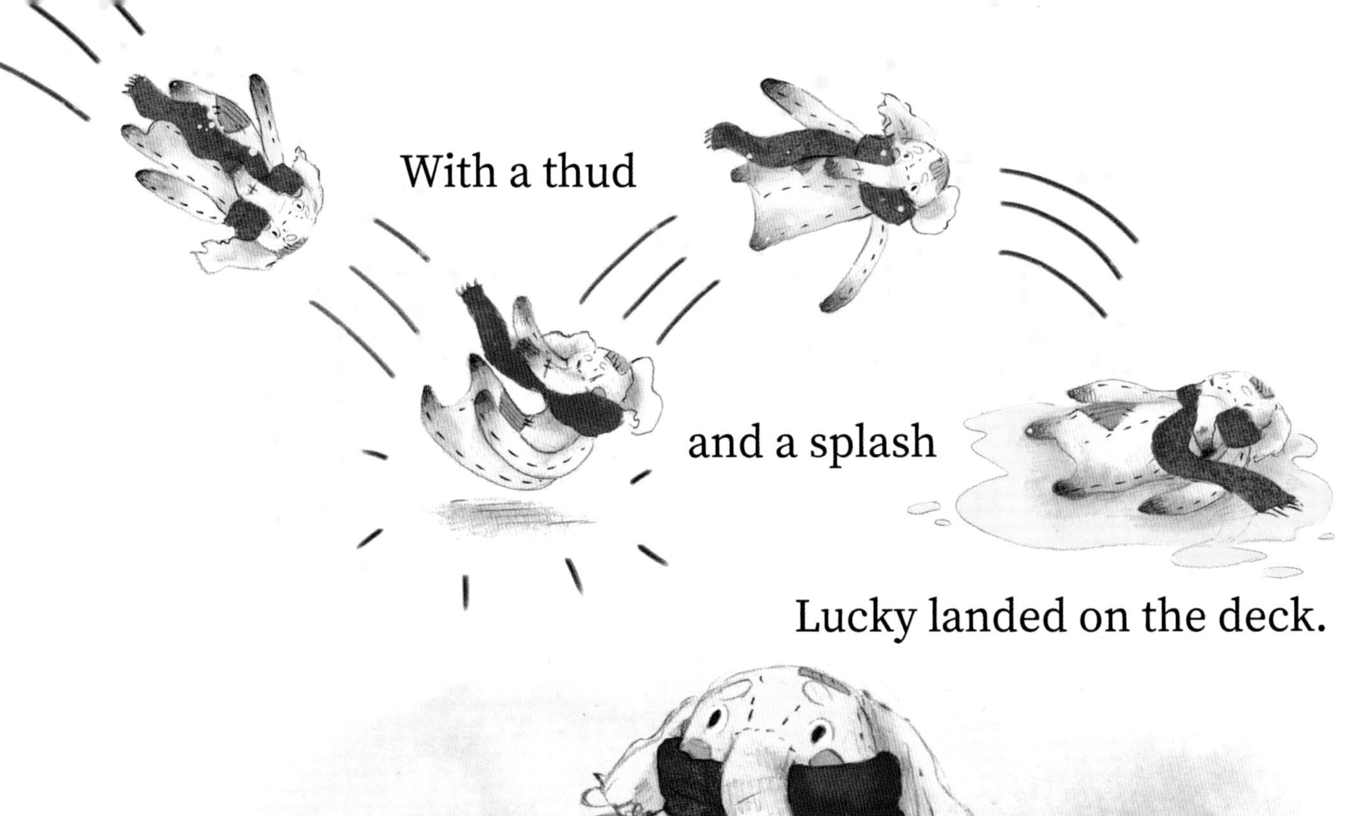

With a thud

and a splash

Lucky landed on the deck.

The captain picked Lucky up from the deck. He was surprised to see a shark swimming near the boat, flapping his fins as if he was waving goodbye.

The captain remembered Lucky and knew just what to do with him.

He turned his boat around, and once back in the port, he tucked Lucky into his satchel and headed toward the little girl's house.

16

The girl's mother answered the door and was surprised to see the sea captain. When he pulled Lucky out of his satchel, she became very excited.

She invited the captain in and brought him over to see the little girl.

The captain held up her favorite toy so she could see him.

"Lucky!" she exclaimed, "You brought him back, Captain. Thank you so much!"

"You've returned from under the sea!"
she said as she hugged her toy.
"You really are Lucky, aren't you!"

"And I am lucky too, because now
I have you back."

The end.

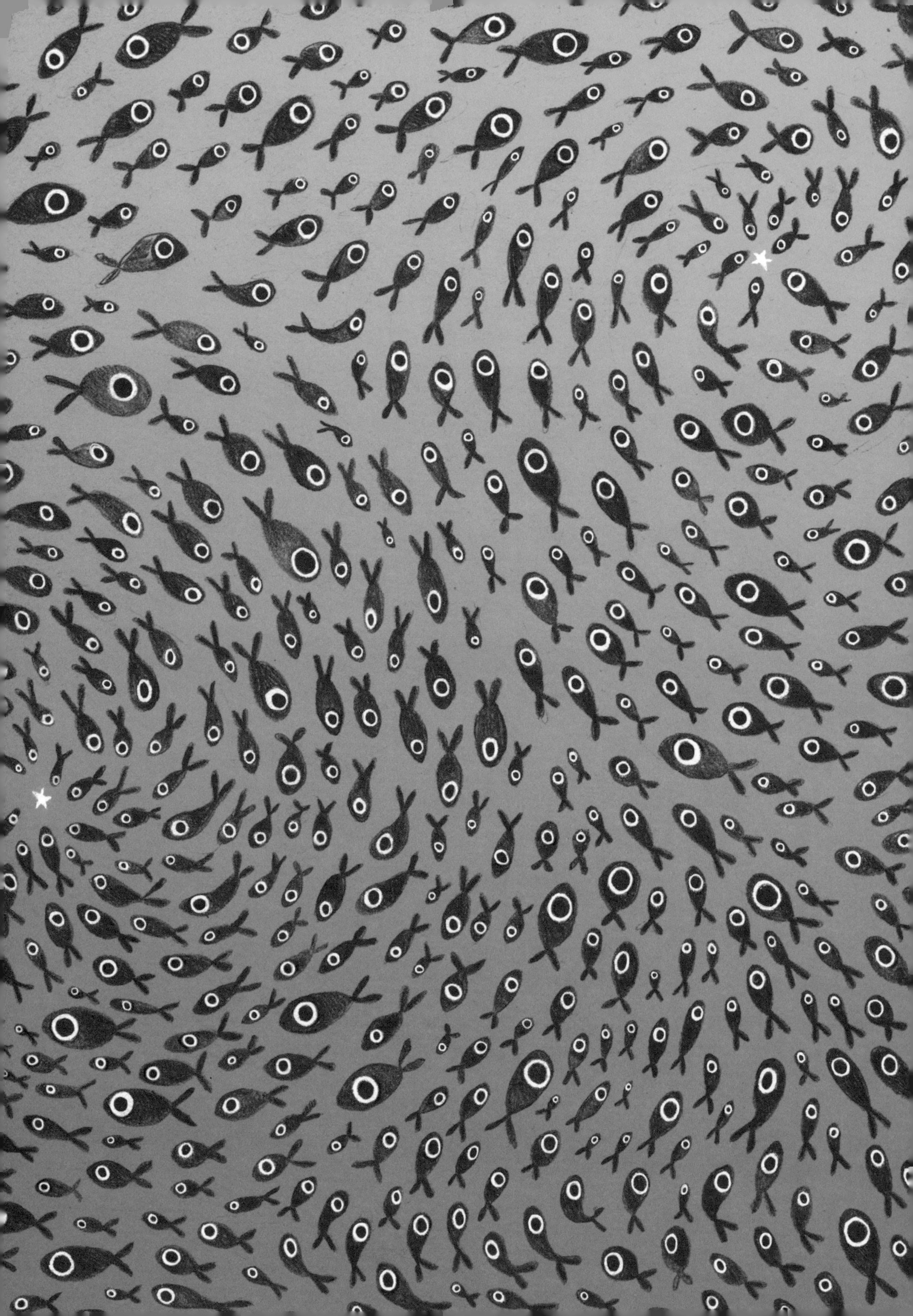